# GROWN-UPS GET TO DO ALL THE DRIVING

# GROWN-UPS GET TO DO ALL THE DRIVING

By William Steig

CAROLRHODA BOOKS, INC. / MINNEAPOLIS

Carolrhoda Books, Inc.
A division of Lerner Publishing Group
241 First Avenue North
Minneapolis, MN 55401 U.S.A.

Website address: www.lernerbooks.com

Library of Congress Cataloging-in-Publication Data

Steig, William, 1907–
Grown-ups get to do all the driving / written and illustrated by
William Steig.
p.    cm.
Summary: A young child lists some of the characteristics and behaviors of grown-ups.
ISBN: 1-57505-617-8 (lib. bdg. : alk. paper)
[1. Adulthood—Fiction.] I. Title.
PZ7.S8177 Gr  2003
[E]—dc21        2002154240

Manufactured in the United States of America
1 2 3 4 5 6 — JR — 08 07 06 05 04 03

For Holly McGhee

GROWN-UPS WANT CHILDREN TO BE HAPPY

GROWN-UPS LIKE TO PUNISH PEOPLE

GROWN-UPS MAKE YOU GO TO THE DENTIST

GROWN-UPS LIKE HANDS TO BE CLEAN

GROWN-UPS ARE ALWAYS WEIGHING THEMSELVES

GROWN-UPS ALWAYS HAVE TO KNOW WHAT TIME IT IS

GROWN-UPS MEASURE EVERYTHING

GROWN-UPS DO LOTS OF EXERCISE

GROWN-UPS CAN'T RUN

GROWN-UPS GET TIRED EASILY

GROWN-UPS TAKE LIBERTIES

GROWN-UPS LOVE RESTAURANTS

GROWN-UPS LIKE PARTIES

GROWN-UPS LIKE TO SLEEP LATE

GROWN-UPS LIKE TO WATCH OTHER PEOPLE PLAY

GROWN-UPS ARE ALWAYS HAVING "DISCUSSIONS"

GROWN-UPS HOG THE TELEPHONE

GROWN-UPS WANT TO KNOW

WHAT'S GOING ON IN THE WHOLE WORLD

GROWN-UPS HATE TO ANSWER QUESTIONS

GROWN-UPS LIKE CHILDREN TO BE POLITE

GROWN-UPS GET BALD

GROWN-UPS CAN TAKE OUT THEIR TEETH

GROWN-UPS GET HEADACHES

GROWN-UPS GET WRINKLES

GROWN-UPS HIDE THINGS

# GROWN-UPS ARE CHEAPSKATES

GROWN-UPS HATE TO PAY THEIR TAXES

GROWN-UPS TAKE A LOT OF PILLS

GROWN-UPS GET TO DO ALL THE DRIVING